THE VAGR

Front cover image by Adobe stock
Book design by Marko Markovic, 5mediadesign

Printed by ColdRock Arts, in the United States of America.

First printing edition 2023

Coldrock Entertainment Arts, Inc.
578 Washington Blvd #1174
Marina del Rey, CA 90292

www.ColdrockArts.com

THE VAGRANT

A SCARY HORROR TALE (SHORT STORY)

by
ED DIAMANTE

THE SLAYER ANTHOLOGY

A **ColdRock** PRODUCTION
ARTS

Dreams died slowly at the Fairfax Gardens.

Or so it seemed as I moved in.

"The place is damned," I heard someone say. I looked back.

A vagrant—shrouded in a dark hoodie and trench coat—was glaring at me from behind the complex gates.

Had he said it?

But I was just a letters and numbers guy with no time for nonsense. Things either added up and made sense, or they didn't. The Fairfax Gardens rent was cheap, and it was month-to-month. The cost savings of living in my new, dumpy apartment was what I needed to get back on my feet, to rebuild my life, to revive my career, all to overcome the worst rut of my life.

As the days turned into weeks, I instead withdrew deeper into myself and my plight. Unable to sleep, I would roam the area late at night every night. My recent breakup had me reeling in a dark place. It had also manifested into writer's block. Something fatal in my line of work. Every time I sat down to write, it came out as a letter to her.

My plots devolved into schemes to win her back. The antagonists I hunted, tortured, and murdered were the guy with which she had cuckolded me. My book was due at the publisher, and I had nothing but disjointed musings and convoluted ramblings. Maybe the publishing house had been right about my having to get out of L.A. and out of my head, to start anew elsewhere, perhaps in New York.

But those 3:00AM L.A. streets pulled me back into the moment and coaxed me to stay. That rare silence made life in L.A. still somewhat bearable. For all its flaws, I still loved the City of Angels, and I still loved her. As unrequited as it all was, I refused to retreat and run away.

I RETURNED TO THE FAIRFAX GARDENS BEFORE DAWN, AS I TYPICALLY DID.

The vagrant was lurking around, scrutinizing the complex as if casing it. Various stray dogs were roaming around, seemingly eyeing the complex as well. I was too broke to move, so I didn't dwell on it. I had bigger problems. I had to sleep and then again attempt to write. The termination of my publishing contract was likely imminent for missing deadline after deadline. I needed a miracle.

A HIDEOUS CACKLE WOKE ME HOURS LATER.

I sat up, realizing I had fallen asleep on the couch instead of writing.

Sleeping in the living room reminded me less of her; the bed always felt too empty.

I groggily rubbed my eyes. It seemed like late afternoon outside. Another wasted day. No writing done, again—

A sudden pounding at the door made me flinch and jump to my feet. I angrily cracked open the door to a smiling young woman I'd never seen before. The stray dogs could be heard barking like crazy outside the complex.

"**Woo-hoo, look at you**, sleepy head. I live across the way. I'm Sistine."

Before I could respond, she nudged her way in, to my dismay.

"Your apartment has new paint!"

My place was a dump, new paint or not.

She seemed quite young, no older than 20 or so. And whatever entered her mind seemed to just come out her mouth.

"I'm in the middle of something," I mentioned. "I work from home—"

"What do you do?"

"Uh…"

She was quite forward, and I was still half asleep and annoyed, and I didn't care how pretty she was.

"Several things," I snapped angrily. "Most of 'em legal."

Her eyes almost squinted to a close, and her shoulders bounced while she laughed uncontrollably yet silently. Her teeth were flawless and pearly-white. She was radiant. The beauty and optimism of her youth had not yet been extinguished by adult life. I was suddenly self-conscious about the dark circles that had developed beneath my eyes and my likely rancid breath—

"Woo-hoo, look at you. So secretive," she replied as she casually walked around the apartment while occasionally gazing at me.

"I'm just a letters and numbers guy—"

"You're good at numbers?"

"Used to be. And letters too..." I lamented, mostly to myself, about my terrible writer's block.

But I stopped myself from saying more. As seductive and disarming as she was, she would not be getting into my head. I was still a wreck after being eviscerated recently by my divorce, after unknowingly finding myself common-law married to my ex, whom I'd been living with since college. She had cleaned me out financially after cheating and then broadsiding me with a no-fault divorce. I then lost what was left in high-risk stock options trading, irrationally attempting to recoup my losses from the divorce—

"Once good at something, you're always good at that something!" Sistine assured me. "Like riding a bike, yeah?"

"I used to be good at things…" I pondered aloud solemnly.

Sistine got up close to me while gazing into my eyes.

"I'm trying to move out of my mom's place—over across the way—and get out of here. Far away from the Fairfax Gardens. But all I have is a few hundred. I know they say the odds of winning the lottery suck, but I'm desperate to get out."

That's why she was here: money.

"I'm no financial advisor," I replied.

"So, I'm going to buy a bunch of lottery tickets. If I lose, I'm still leaving, and I'll figure it out later".

"You're going to gamble away; what little money you have?"

Her plan was so ridiculous it grated me. I went against my better judgment and blurted out before I could stop myself, "If you insist on going high-risk, there's an up-and-coming company I'm watching."

She just stared at me blankly.

"As in the stock market. The company reports earnings next week. The stock price will likely spike since they'll likely report profitability for the first time. That's when you sell. If it doesn't work out, at least you'll own the stock shares to go long instead since the company has big, long-term growth potential; it's solidly breaking even now and has no debt, so it won't go belly up anytime soon. A price spike is better odds than buying lottery tickets, especially since it's currently trading well under a dollar."

Her eyes squinted to a close as her shoulders bounced while laughing uncontrollably yet silently, "I didn't understand anything you just said."

I grabbed a pen and wrote the stock's three-letter ticker symbol on her palm—

Sistine moved closer, gave me a wet kiss, and whispered, "I'll do anything to escape Mother".

She ran out of there, with me dazed.

What the…?

My surprise was exceeded by shocked fright as seconds later, a crazy-eyed woman stormed into the apartment, clutching Sistine by the arm while screaming at me in absolute rage.

"Stay away from my daughter, you pervert! Or the last thing you'll see before it goes black will be her face!"

"What?"

"You know damn well you're playing with danger!"

"Danger? The stock market?" I replied, perplexed.

"Don't play stupid! You've been here long enough to hear the demon my daughter and I are at war with! Stay away from her!"

Demon? What the hell was this crazy lady talking about? No wonder Sistine was hellbent on moving out. To get away from her toxic, abusive mother, whose name I later found out to be Lilith. She shoved Sistine out of my apartment and slammed the door shut behind them.

I stood there in shock, clutching my head in disbelief. I pondered calling the cops, but Sistine was an adult—taller and seemingly stronger than her mother—so surely she could leave whenever she wanted.

I decided to stay out of it since what I really needed was to get my life back in order. So as to get the hell out of the Fairfax Gardens, away from all the crazies that seemed to be coming out of the woodwork. My objective was singular, and I would NOT be deterred.

BUT I AGAIN FAILED TO BREAK MY WRITER'S BLOCK AND WANDERED THE 3:00 AM streets again that night, trying to clear my head and instead brooding over the burning turd my life had become. That insurmountable rut and downward spiral left me consumed by a nauseating sense of impending doom as I felt myself descending into illness—both physical and mental. I was dreadfully counting down the last days to my deadline, days numbered by the looming inevitability of my contract termination at the publishing house for another missed deadline.

I arrived back at the Fairfax Gardens after dawn as I typically did, bent on bypassing sleep to make another attempt to write. But as I approached my apartment, the vagrant was there, glaring at me.

"This place is damned," he grunted.

I calmly walk past him, unsure how he got into the complex. The gates were always locked.

"You must leave," he ordered.

"We each make our own hell and lie in it," I replied as I opened my apartment door and entered.

"Why else do you think the complex is near-empty?" he said. "People *get* their wish around here."

The vagrant stood at my door as I closed it.

"STAY AWAY FROM HER," he barked through the door.

Stay away from *who*?

The pieces suddenly fell together. A surge of paranoid rage hit me.

"Did my ex-wife hire you to harass me?! Isn't it enough she took everything?! She wants my sanity too?!" I yelled back.

I furiously opened the door, clutching my kitchen knife.

But the vagrant was gone.

I slammed the door shut and paced around the apartment for a while.

I sat at my desk eventually and fought back a sob.

I had gotten soft, weak, useless. I'd forgotten that writing was a job, that breakthroughs were hard-fought and taken by brute force when necessary. The notion of an artist waiting and hoping for inspiration to strike was a naïve fantasy. Nothing in life was free. Everything was a slog.

I recommitted to the fact that my ONLY escape from the Fair-fax Gardens would be through my writing. Like any prisonbreak, it would not be easy. It was either that or die. So, I tuned out the world by switching on some classical music and raising the volume to the max. I closed my eyes to focus. I gradually began typing away at my laptop computer. Slow at first, then faster and faster until my fingers banged away furiously at the keyboard. I was venting aimlessly. It was all coming out as a grievance letter to my ex-wife, then suddenly veered toward what seemed like a complaint to the police explaining all the illegalities being inflicted upon me. One way or another, all the harassment was going to stop! I was livid, and I poured out my rage, my heart, my soul into the narrative.

As I typed, I found a familiar solace.

I had always worked out life's problems in writing, as I was doing there and then, systematically using narrative, logic, and math to navigate the void in search of a solution. It was how my mind was wired, and it was how I wrote my stories. A novel was where the messiness of human nature, structural narrative engineering, thematic poetry, and raw artistic license all coalesced. That had manifested in a successful writing career and wealth amplification via my stock investments. I had tasted success early in life, but my safe, orderly methodologies had stopped working. Things had gotten insurmountably out of whack. Chaos had engulfed me. Everything had been upended. I'd never taken overly excessive risks, but the old ways no longer worked. I was spiraling more and more toward increased recklessness. My nightly walks and budding attraction to Sistine were perhaps a symptom of those increasing flirtations with trouble. It was likely a desperate attempt to serendipitously cure my life's ills since the numbers no longer added up, since the narratives no longer worked, all as my writing floundered while the bearish stock market mauled to death what was left of my wealth. Letters and numbers had betrayed me. I was adrift with no true north and no sail. I had nothing left, and no recourse as my life had long degenerated into silent desperation.

My written rant eventually morphed into some kind of manifesto about not only what was wrong with my life but what was wrong with society and humanity. I felt myself slipping into an envious hatred of those who were more successful. They surely were at fault for the disaster my life had become. I was possessed more and more by a jealous rage as I boiled in the caldron of venom where the worst scourges of human existence were forged; there in the caustic stew of sociopathic degeneracy where those who hated their own lives chose to instead "fix" the world rather than themselves. My manifesto had blown out of the gates of hell and had landed somewhere between Karl Marx and Mein Kampf: the two biggest catalysts for industrial-scale mass murder the world had ever seen.

I stopped and clutched my face.

That was NOT who I was.

I harbored no envious rage or hatred toward anyone.

I had never blamed or demonized others for my failures.

What was happening to me?

After so many hours of writing, this's what I had created?

I wept as I slowly emerged from the depths of hell, rejecting hate.

I instead slowly refocused, searched my soul, and gradually remolded the vitriol into the singular embodiment and personification of virulent evil, then sugarcoated it with charm and beauty and self-proclaimed moral virtue so as to rebrand that toxic rot into candy for the masses. That was the huge breakthrough I'd been desperately pursuing for months: the antagonist of my new novel had been born.

As hours gave way to days of more excruciation, out of the ashes of my dwindling sanity arose my new yet deeply flawed protagonist, as well as that main character's redemptive journey to stop the evil antagonist.

My new novel was finally taking form.

As days gave way to weeks of escalating excruciation, while the classical music blasted so as to tune out the world, I engineered the formative years of both my protagonist and antagonist and the inevitability of their collision course. Their escalating skirmishes manifested via the elaborate intertwining of plot, subplot, characterization, character arc, dueling points of view and theme, subliminal motifs, and the numerous other moving parts that make a novel. I clawed back my inner demons as I engineered theirs; their fears, their failures, their traumas, their wounds, their conscious and unconscious desires, their darkest hours, and how it all had warped their worldviews. Both my protagonist and antagonist were as broken as me, but over the course of their turbulent journey, as their clashes grew increasingly fiery, only one would transcend their demons and survive to obtain what they wanted.

As I wrote, I laughed, I cried, I raged like a madman, for such was the life of a writer—one is what one writes. And as the story's journey neared its end, I came to forgive myself for all my failings, and I forgave my ex-wife and the guy with which she cucked me. At my novel's climatic end, I forgave the world for all perceived grievances and injustices as the old me died along with my virulently evil antagonist. Just then—

To my DISMAY…

My antagonist rose from the ashes and DEFEATED my protagonist in a sudden double-twist, producing a superior and more satisfying ending.

The bad guy had won!

I stood and slowly backed away from the computer. What the fuck?

I shut off the classical music and paced around.

I fervently resumed writing, more focused than ever.

But the more I tried to rework and rewrite the story and the ending, the more exhausted and ill I felt. My will was proving unable to kill my virulently evil antagonist. Instead, my heroic main character-protagonist lay dead and could not be resurrected to rise from the ashes as well, so as to win in the end via some ironic, triple-twist masterpiece of some kind. I was not a good enough author to execute my ambitions for the story, which was that good ALWAYS prevailed in the end.

I had failed and eventually succumbed to the will of my evil book.

I collapsed, too exhausted to continue the battle.

My antagonist—the embodiment of all my demons and flaws and rage and wrath and everything tragically wrong with me as a human being and, quite possibly, everything wrong with all human beings—stood victorious and laughing diabolically. Hate had won.

A virulent evil had been unleashed upon the world, and I had been its conduit. What I had written was a despicable lie. I knew it down to every fiber of my being. I decided to delete it all and start over...after a brief rest...

A HIDEOUS ROAR SHOOK ME.

I awoke on the floor beside my desk.

The roar again raged, "It's mine!".

I stumbled to my feet.

The clock read 3:00AM.

I realized it was my first time sleeping through the night in the apartment since moving in. Normally, I'd be roaming the nighttime streets to clear my head or, more recently, fervently typing away all night while blasting classical music—

Wait, that goddamned book. I was going to delete it. I stood in order to do just that—

There was a sudden pounding at my door.

I flinched but then rushed the door angrily, refusing to be harassed and tormented anymore by that degenerate vagrant.

As I opened the door, Lilith—Sistine's crazy mother—charged in and threw two handfuls of cash in my face.

I jumped back as she screamed at the top of her lungs.

"You son of a bitch! Did you give that money to my daughter?!"

I had never seen anyone so enraged.

"You pervert! Sistine is 19 and too young for you, you low life!"

"I didn't give anybody anything!" I finally mustered.

"How the hell did she get thousands of dollars?!"

I clutched my head in disbelief as it dawned on me that...

"She actually bought my stock tip? Good for her—"

Lilith landed a scalding slap to my face.

"YOU HAVE NO IDEA WHAT YOU'RE MESSING WITH! Stay the hell away from my daughter! Mind your own damn business; you don't know anything about her and her special needs!"

Lilith stormed out.

I stood there in my living room in shock, clutching my aching face. It was clearer than ever that Sistine was a prisoner to her abusive mother.

I rushed after Lilith, but the vagrant was outside the complex gates glaring at me menacingly, wagging his finger: NO. As if I were some idiot child. A large blade seemed to shimmer from inside the opening in his coat. The dogs were howling. My heart sank. No wonder Sistine wanted so badly the hell out. She was in grave danger because everyone around her was out of their minds. I was going to get the hell out of the Fairfax Gardens, but I could not leave Sistine behind to die.

I RESUMED MY NIGHTLY WALKS AS IF NOTHING HAD HAPPENED.

It was my way of not signaling my intentions to escape with Sistine. Mostly, I was subtly casing the inside and outside of the complex every time I came and went. But like a predator stalking prey, the vagrant always seemed to be glaring at the complex from the opening of his cardboard box shelter across the street. He was never camped at the same spot twice. The dogs likewise never stayed long in a single spot and never seemed to take their menacing sights off the complex as they roamed around. It was as if they had something cornered inside the complex. I just needed the hell out and didn't care to know what was happening with all that.

Instead, I was increasingly focused on planning a move to New York. I was done with L.A., and its soft weather, its superficialities, its worsening vagrancy, its increasing insanity. It was bringing out the worse in me. Perhaps New York's mauling cold, its suffocating summer humidity, its realer people, and the drastic change it offered could help restore my well-being, perhaps even offer me a chance to reinvent myself. But had never fled my demons; instead, I had always confronted them. I needed to close out my L.A. life before leaving. Departing L.A. had to be on my own terms, not some cowardly retreat, I had decided. And how was I going to fund it all?

A MACABRE CACKLE WOKE ME.

I stumbled out of bed. I assumed it had been a nightmare.

A beam of sunlight was permeating through a crack in the blinds suggesting it was afternoon.

I flinched as the phone rang.

I answered it.

It was my agent.

She informed me that they loved the book.

What book? I hadn't even sent out my new book to anyone. Had I?

No, quite the opposite; I was going to delete the damn thing.

I rushed to my computer to check what the hell was going on as my agent boasted about having started a bidding war at the major publishing houses. That was impossible on all levels, firstly because I had not sent it to her, but mostly like Hemingway said: "The first draft of anything is shit."

Just then, I dropped the phone upon seeing the sent email to my agent...with the book file attached. No subject, no message, just the file.

My evil had been unleashed into the world! But how?

I had no recollection of sending it. Surely...it hadn't sent itself? I grabbed my phone off the floor, but before I could warn her—

"...the best offer thus far is a one-million dollar advance," she said.

A macabre cackle made me flinch. I look around frantically. I was losing my mind. I needed the hell out of the Fairfax Gardens fast.

"I accept," I responded, not caring about the details. "I'm getting the hell out of L.A. and coming to you guys in New York."

I hung up while assuring myself I'd fix the book in coordination with the publishing house editor. I was going to kill my evil antagonist, hell or high water, deus ex-machina if necessary: the gravest of all writing sins—

There was a pounding at my front door. What the hell?

I rushed to the door and opened it.

Sistine barged in and shut the door behind her, locking it and leaning against it as if trying to keep something out. The dogs could be heard howling.

"Woo-hoo, look at you," she casually said with a mischievous smile.

"Uh…"

"I'm leaving. Like today," she said.

"Leaving?"

"I'm finally moving out, like I told you."

"Right, yes, of course," I said, still reeling from the avalanche of everything seemingly happening at once, but I managed to get it together fast. "Good! Really good! Yes, get out of here. This place is batshit crazy."

I was relieved she was getting out before me. One less thing for me to worry about.

"But I think you have something of mine, though?" she said.

"I do?"

"My mom… I'm so embarrassed. I'm so sorry."

"Right! The money she threw in my face. Your money from the stock trade!" I happily grabbed the cash from the kitchen drawer and handed it to her.

She hugged me tight. I slowly hugged back.

"Go on. Run on out of here," I said.

"I don't want this to be goodbye," she sighed.

"Don't worry about me. I'm moving to New York. To start over in a new place."

She continued holding me tight.

"I think maybe I need to start over in a new place too," she whispered.

Presumptuous or not, right or wrong, I wanted her.

"Get your stuff and meet me back here fast to load my car. I'm leaving most everything behind," I said.

"Woo-hoo, look at you."

"Are you safe to get your stuff?"

"Mother and I have a new understanding," Sistine replied ominously and kissed me, lightly slipping her tongue into my mouth, then ran out.

The *right* girl had destroyed me in every way; perhaps the wrong girl was not all that wrong. Sistine felt and tasted so right. New York awaited.

I rushed to the adjacent carport, where my old clunker was parked. I loaded into the trunk a suitcase with my clothes and a backpack with my work materials and laptop. That was all I was taking.

I rushed back to the apartment. My heart sank.

The vagrant was standing in my living room instead of Sistine.

"Why was the girl here?" he said menacingly.

He looked taller and more foreboding than ever.

"Are you stalking us?" I replied.

"Why was she here?!" he raged.

I glimpsed the shimmer of the large blade on him through the opening in his coat. I fled to Sistine's rather than my car.

The vagrant furiously ran after me.

"No, Goddamn you!" he raged.

I stormed into Lilith & Sistine's apartment but was pummeled by a kaleidoscopic stench of roses and rot. I keeled over, gagging, then frantically cowered back at the sight of Lilith's headless corpse sitting on the sofa, legs casually crossed.

Lilith's maggot-covered head was on the coffee table beside scattered cans of rose air freshener. The eyes were gone.

The vagrant rushed into the apartment after me, unfazed by the horror.

"Why did you do this?!" I screamed at him.

"Leave this place!" the vagrant ordered as he calmly assessed the situation. "Or she will do the same to you."

"AMBROSE!" a hideous roar shook the walls. "What took you so long to come and face me?"

The vagrant coolly drew his long blade and stood in a defensive stance as if readying for something to come at him.

"Get out! Now!" the vagrant yelled at me. Just then—

Sistine scurried in on all fours and pounced on the vagrant with animalistic speed.

"Woo-hoo! Look at you!" Sistine roared while clawing at him as he covered his face with his arms.

I ran out of there, never more horrified, unsure of what I saw or what was happening.

"Wait for me!" Sistine roared.

I ran straight for my car, never looking back.

I jumped in and peeled out of the carport.

But Sistine jumped in front of the car, clutching a small suitcase.

I slammed the brakes.

She looked normal again.

I didn't know what to believe as my frayed mind teetered on the brink.

Sistine ran to the passenger side, opened the door, and jumped in as she tossed her suitcase into the back seat.

"Let's go! He's coming!" Sistine pleaded. Her nose was bleeding; the vagrant had clearly beaten her. I slammed my foot on the accelerator, caring only for her safety. Just then—

I could see the vagrant in the rearview mirror sprinting after the car and gaining fast.

He punched his fist through the rear passenger window and held on as I sped away.

The vagrant swiftly climbed in through the broken window and into the back seat, gun in hand, like some professional assassin.

"Ambrose!" Sistine screamed, "Leave me alone!"

"You know this guy?!" I screamed.

"He is a murderous slayer!" she cried.

"*Slayer*? Of what—"

"Do as I say, or I'll kill you both," the vagrant calmly ordered, not so much as breathing hard or sweating despite all that had happened.

"Why you doing this?!" I pleaded.

"Things like *her* do not exist. Because things like her are eradicated. By us," he rasped.

In the rearview mirror, I saw the dogs chasing after the car until we eventually left them long behind.

THE VAGRANT HAD ME DRIVE DEEP INTO THE SANTA MONICA MOUNTAINS at gunpoint. These idyllic mountains, remote in some places, separated L.A.'s Valley from the ocean. I noticed birds darting out of trees as if unable to flee us fast enough. I didn't give it another thought as my heart sank when it became evident that the wilderness was the perfect place for murder.

"Look, I'm sure this's some big misunderstanding," I pleaded with him, deciding it was time to act or die trying. "At least, let her go—"

"You saw what she did to her own mother," the vagrant grunted.

"I'm not sure what I saw—"

"*You* killed my mother, *Ambrose*," she coolly said as if mocking him.

"How could you?" I asked the vagrant.

He angrily jammed the gun barrel into the base of my skull.

"She's a witch," the vagrant growled. "The most powerful one we've ever encountered, a living conduit to hell. She's an abominate, and even animals know it!"

The vagrant was clearly just another mentally ill homeless person, delusional and wandering the streets of L.A. unmedicated and unhelped.

"I have money," I blurted. "It's yours if you let us go."

"Money," the vagrant grunted, unimpressed. "That's what she got you."

"Got me?"

"Unlike you, the mother at least had integrity, as she foolishly refused our help, choosing to go it alone to try to save her daughter—"

"She was holding Sistine prisoner!"

"To contain the evil!" the vagrant growled. "But the mother was in over her head and paid for it with her life."

"I'll PAY for your psychiatric treatment and anything else you need—"

"Any good fortunes you recently came upon are NOT yours!" the vagrant roared. "At least the mother had enough integrity not to sell out!"

"What are you talking about?!"

"This witch has a talent for granting wishes," the vagrant said. "By selling peoples' souls to Satan on their behalf...so their wishes come true."

I was at a loss for words.

"On top of demon-conjuring, curses, and other witchcraft," the vagrant added.

"Why?"

"Because the Devil wants souls. And Sistine delivers them to him."

The letters and numbers and potential solutions whirled in my head.

"Every penny I ever made in my life, I earned," my ego compelled me to say. Anything short of that was humiliating to me.

"Please don't let him hurt me," Sistine begged me.

"Only *we* are equipped to handle situations like *hers*," the vagrant told me menacingly, his eyes warning me that he would not hesitate to kill me.

"What do you intend to do to her?" I asked, unable to stop myself.

"We will break all her pacts with Satan, emancipating your soul and others."

"I won't let you hurt her—"

The vagrant blasted me in the head with his massive fist.

"Time for you to stop the car, get out, and walk back to the city. Don't look back. Maybe, just maybe, you won't burn in hell for eternity."

My mind and heart raced as a gut-wrenching CHOICE became evident.

No way I was giving back my book, my cash advance, or Sistine. I was just a numbers and letters guy, and though nothing added up or made sense anymore, I was prepared to accept my new reality. Damnation or not, Sistine and I were going to make a life together in New York. I accepted that she was my muse and enchantress. And I somehow knew she would make all things right.

I violently swerved the car straight into a tree while flooring the gas pedal since the vagrant was the only one in the car not wearing a seatbelt.

"Woo-hoo! Look at you!"

It all went black.

I AWAKENED IN A HOSPITAL BED.

The recollections swirling in my frayed mind felt impossible to believe.

Had it all really happened?

After they told me no one else was found in the wreck, I agreed I must've fallen asleep at the wheel, knowing damn well that wasn't what happened.

I was released after an overnight observation for my concussion and bruised ribs. I never returned to the Fairfax Gardens as I instead rushed straight to the airport via taxi. My agent had made all the arrangements, including my reservation at a Midtown Manhattan hotel, where I would stay until I found an apartment.

To my dismay, upon my arrival, they had put me up in the penthouse suite. Courtesy of the publishing house. My agent said I was the publisher's flavor of the month. That's how much they had loved the book proposal, as they called it. I wasted no time diving into a second draft to kill my evil antagonist while considering their developmental editing notes. According to my agent, we were going to make lots of money, and there was already talk about film rights. I enjoyed the complimentary champagne and caviar as I wrote, at my fancy desk, in the posh study of the opulent penthouse.

After a soak in the hot tub, while enjoying a second bottle of champagne, I went to sleep on the luxurious king-size bed. Life was grand, and I now had most everything I'd ever wanted.

I WAS SHAKEN OUT OF BED BY A BLOOD-CURDLING SHRIEK AT 3:00AM.

Unfazed, I eagerly approached the front door of the penthouse and opened it without hesitation, somehow knowing full well who it was.

"Woo-hoo, look at you," Sistine casually said as she strolled in, admiring the place, and looking more beautiful than ever, dressed in a long, snug, flowing, black dress.

I felt no need to ask her how she found me and why she looked more stunning than ever. I took Sistine into my arms, kissed her ravenously, and then carried her to my bed.

The letters and numbers did not add up, and the narrative did not work. None of it made sense, and I didn't care. There was no doubt everything the vagrant—Slayer Ambrose—had said was true. I was not naïve enough to believe otherwise. This was all a dream come true, but "dreams come true" did not just fall from the sky. I had not earned any of this, not yet and not at this scale, yet I happily accepted it. And so the transaction was complete. I had fully sold out. My soul, in exchange for all of this, had been successfully brokered by my beloved muse and enchantress, Sistine. I was not blameless in any of it nor any of its eventualities. I even rationalized it as taking back what was rightfully mine, what was taken from me in the divorce. So be it. My beloved Sistine, my muse, my angel witch, my imminent destruction, my eternal damnation. Woo-hoo, look at us as we fucked all night amid breathtaking views of the Manhattan skyline through the penthouse glass walls of the master bedroom. That would be as close to heaven as I would ever get. The reckoning awaited; if not tomorrow, the next day, next month, next year, or next decade, the light at the end of my tunnel would indeed be hell.

THE END

For other SLAYER ANTHOLOGY

short stories and novels, please visit:

Printed in Great Britain
by Amazon

58931856R00030